Dear Parents,

Welcome to the Scholastic Reader series. We have taken over ... years of experience with teachers, parents, and children and put it into a program that is designed to match your child's interests and skills.

Level 1—Short sentences and stories made up of words kids can sound out using their phonics skills and words that are important to remember.

Level 2—Longer sentences and stories with words kids need to know and new "big" words that they will want to know.

Level 3—From sentences to paragraphs to longer stories, these books have large "chunks" of text and are made up of a rich vocabulary.

Level 4—First chapter books with more words and fewer pictures.

It is important that children learn to read well enough to succeed in school and beyond. Here are ideas for reading this book with your child:

- Look at the book together. Encourage your child to read the title and make a prediction about the story.
- Read the book together. Encourage your child to sound out words when appropriate. When your child struggles, you can help by providing the word.
- Encourage your child to retell the story. This is a great way to check for comprehension.

Scholastic Readers are designed to support your child's efforts to learn how to read at every age and every stage. Enjoy helping your child learn to read and love to read.

      —Francie Alexander
        Chief Education Officer
        Scholastic Education

Ms. Frizzle

Liz

Written by Martin Schwabacher.
Illustrated by Carolyn Bracken.

Based on *The Magic School Bus* books
written by Joanna Cole and illustrated by Bruce Degen.

The author and editor would like to thank Carl Mehlina and Sean Mortha
of the American Museum of Natural History, New York City,
for their expert advice in preparing this manuscript.

0-439-80106-0

30 29 28 27 26 25 24   40   13 14 15/0

Designed by Rick DeMonico.

Printed in the U.S.A.   First printing, September 2005

The Magic School Bus®
FLIES WITH THE DINOSAURS

Arnold   Ralphie   Keesha   Phoebe   Carlos   Tim   Wanda   Dorothy Ann

Cartwheel
·B·O·O·K·S·®

SCHOLASTIC INC.

New York   Toronto   London   Auckland   Sydney
Mexico City   New Delhi   Hong Kong   Buenos Aires

It's fun to be in Ms. Frizzle's class.
Her dresses are strange.
Her shoes are strange.

PTEROSAUR

DINOSAUR

BIRD

OUR BUS IS STRANGE.

D.A. says her favorite dinosaur is her pet parrot, Dinah!

"A parrot is not a dinosaur!" Ralphie says.

"It's a bird," Tim agrees.

D.A. tells us that the first birds were small dinosaurs with feathers.

"Did birds really come from dinosaurs?"
Carlos asks.
Ms. Frizzle gets that funny look in her eyes.
"Let's look for clues!" she says.

The bus drives along.
Soon, we see some dinosaurs.

JINZHOUSAURUS

Ms. Frizzle drives after the pterosaur.
"Let's get a closer look," she says.

The bus slows down. We see some small dinosaurs.
They are sitting on eggs.

THOSE LOOK LIKE BIRD EGGS.

CAUDIPTERYX

"No," Ms. Frizzle says. "They have arms, not wings.
And they use their feathers to keep warm, not to fly."

SINORNITHOSAURUS

Arnold sees the dinosaur just in time.
It has fuzzy, fluffy feathers that look
like fur.
It also has claws! And it eats meat!
The Friz says it can't fly, but it jumps
right at us!

YIKES!

YIKES!

YIKES!

We climb into the tree.
Then we see a strange bird.
It has wings, and it can fly.
But it also has teeth and a long tail!

MICRORAPTOR

Now we are flying over China.
We are in our time again.
We see people looking
for dinosaur fossils below.

THE STORY OF FOSSILS
by Arnold

After millions of years,
the ashes turned to rock.
The dinosaur bones
turned to rock, too.
Now they are called fossils.
People find the fossils
and learn about dinosaurs.

MORE ON
BIRDS AND DINOSAURS

The dinosaurs in this book look strange, but they are all real. They were discovered very recently by fossil hunters in Liaoning, China.

These new discoveries were very important. They proved that birds were not the only animals with feathers. Other dinosaurs had feathers, too.

Dinosaur feathers changed over time: First some dinosaurs got soft, short, fluffy feathers. Then some dinosaurs got longer, stiffer feathers. Finally some small dinosaurs used their long, stiff feathers to fly. Some of these dinosaurs were the first birds.

After birds appeared, the earlier feathered dinosaurs did not all die out. Feathered dinosaurs that could not fly lived side by side with birds for millions of years.

That is why all the dinosaurs Ms. Frizzle and the kids see on their trip were living together in China 130 million years ago.

Tyrannosaurus

WHAT DOES A TYRANNOSAURUS REX EAT?